T0144979

TU:
The Astronaut

To order additional copies of this book, contact:
Xlibris
844-714-8691
www.Xlibris.com
Orders@Xlibris.com

ISBN: Softcover   978-1-6698-6822-4
        EBook   978-1-6698-6823-1

Print information available on the last page

Rev. date: 02/22/2023

Tu: The Astronaut

Written By L.C. Cannon

"Tu" said his mother,
" It's time to get up for school,
remember today is career day!"
Tu got up, made his bed.

3

He went into the bathroom.
He washed his face, brushed teeth,
and combed his hair.

He went back into his room.

"Where is it?"
said Tu while searching his closet,
"Ahhh, here it is!"
Tu said with a sigh of relief.

7

Tu dressed himself
and ran down the stairs.

"My, my, don't you look handsome"
says his mother,
"Here's your favorite.PANCAKES!"
Tu loved pancakes.
He ate his breakfast.

Then he headed out to the car.
"Buckle your seatbelt Tu"
Said mom

Finally, Tu was at school.
He kissed his mother,
and went inside.

"Wow!" …….. "Look!"……… "So cool!"
whispers and soft giggles went around the class.
Tu walked in with a big smile across his face.

Miss. Daisy was the 5th grade teacher
at Oak Pear Elementary
and all the students loved her.
She was funny, tall with high cheekbones.
She looked like a model,
and her favorite color was purple.

Today she had on a long white coat
and black pants.
"Can anyone guess what I am?"
Miss. Daisy asked the class.

Nobody raised their hand.

"Well, tough crowd,"
she mocked with a pleasant grin.
"I am a scientist!
I teach you during the day
and work in a science lab at night!"

"Yes.... Cindy?"
"What do you do in the science lab?"
she asked inquisitively.

"I run tests on plants!

Michael, yes,
what is your question?"
"Umm ......What kind of test?
A math test?".

" No dear," she said, giggling.
"I study and experiment on them to
find out the type of plant it is,
what soil makes them grow,that type of stuff.
Pretty boring huh?, but I get to work
with a lot of rare exotic plants.
I'm a botanist,
but enough about me, today I want
to hear about your career!.
Who can tell me what
career means?"

Tu raises his hand,
"A career is the work you decide
to spend the rest of your life doing"
He says with surety.
"That's right!"
agreed Miss. Daisy.

"Would you like to come up
and tell us about your career choice?"
Tu was so excited to share his career with his peers,
He could even
answer three questions about his choice.
He was so ready!

Tu reaches the front of the classroom
He then faces all his classmates.
"Can you guess what I am?"

Nobody raised their hand.

"I'm an astronaut,
I'm the Chief of NASA."

"Yeah, Pedro",
calling on his first classmate for a question.
"Why do you want to be an astronaut?
and What's NASA? " Asked Pedro.
"I want to be an astronaut because spaceships are cool,
they make a lot of money,
and I've always wanted to visit the moon,
oh yeah
NASA is the National Aeronautics
and Space Administration"
Answered Tu.

"Great questions Pedro,
but let's stick to one question only!"
Ms. Daisy said
before Tu called on his next classmate.

"Umm, Joel" Tu said, calling on the next classmate.
" Is being an astronaut a dangerous job?" he asked.
"Sometimes it can be,
There has been a few times
astronauts died in space." He said.

"Lastly.... ummmm.....Dalliaha!"
"I think it's cool", Said Dalliaha.
"Thanks!"
said Tu as he smiled and took his seat.

The day went by pretty fast as his
classmates one after the other
talked about their career choices.
A Teacher,
a Police Officer,
a FireFighter, and
even a Princess.
Everyone seemed to know what they wanted to be
and why.

At dinner, Tu told his mother and father all about
how wonderful career day was.
He told them how everyone reacted to his Spacesuit
and all about how cool his crush,
Dalliaha, thought it was.

"Son, I am so happy you had a great
career day at school"
Said his father.
"Me too!"
Said his mother"
But now that you are finished with your supper,
it is time for bed."

Tu excused himself from the table,
kissed his parents goodnight,
then went upstairs to the bathroom.

He washed his face,
brushed his teeth,
and changed into his bed clothes.

In his bedroom,
Tu pulled back the covers,
got in bed, and fell fast asleep.

He dreamed that he was in a spaceship
Destination, The moon.

The End

Printed in the United States
by Baker & Taylor Publisher Services